The Monarchy

Vihan.R

ISBN 978-93-5667-639-8
© Vihan.R 2023

Published in India 2023 by Pencil

A brand of
One Point Six Technologies Pvt. Ltd.
Unit no. 26, Ground Floor, Building A1,
Wadala Truck Terminal Road,
Near Post Office, Antop Hill, Mumbai - 400037
E connect@thepencilapp.com
W www.thepencilapp.com

Author biography

the authors name is vihan.R he is born in india chennai, and for further contact you can have his email:rajanvihan12@gmail.com

CONTENTS

History 7

seperated 8

into countries of two 9

war 10

revenge 11

poverty 12

blood moon 13

all about the blood moon 14

golems 15

invasion 16

unhappy 17

power 18

n thinks of a scheme 19

team up 20

the scheme 21

betrayal 22

locked up 23

Ar joins 24

escape route 25

mini betrayal 26

better betrayal 27

stranded on an island 28

back to home 29

thinking of what to do to n 30

knowing 31

serial killer 32

playing a game 33

peace love and war 34

endbreak 35

a new era 36

History

Once there were about 6 powerful brave people who could have ruled the earth but chose not to.

N, ni, v, r, a, ar, all were very powerful that no one could stand a chance against them. N was a very strong man who was good in hunting, searching, guarding and many more things. Then Ni was very skilled at running away, hiding, targeting, has a sharp eyesight and more. V was a skilled swordsman, archery kind of guy, and anything that has fighting with it, he is also a very kind man who would sacrifice his life for the country. R is very good in the inventory section, carpenter, and fighting with spears, and searching for anything needed. A was the same thing as r but more experienced, and a always charges into battle to protect. And the youngest of them all, ar who only knew fighting and guarding, a little bit. But these 6 were unstoppable.

seperated

Separated

Most of the people wanted to have different countries because those liked a few as leaders and others were unhappy with the king N. So, we let them have their way, we had to split into two countries that had been separated with a big wall. But there were the six who had to choose between the two countries. N, A, and Ar choose one side, and Ni, V and R choose the other.

into countries of two

The country v was part of was named merndend, and the other was named ruynery. Merndend was having the 3 who joined as their kings, and same for ruynery. When the kings had a meeting, they all discussed.
War

war

During the meeting those who had argued were short temperd due to the problem, but due to both countries' crisis, they couldn't see themselves over their oppositions, so ni took ar as hostage. The move he had made broke into war, ruynery's army killed many innocent people. Because of this, v murdered atleast 100 people with r killing 86. After ar being taken by hostage, ruynery found ar and ni. they rescued ar and took ni as hostage. Once v and r came back, they saw ni being stabbed by bones all around him and wondered why. Then he just realized that this is also a world of magics. Ni was thrown in the jail, along with r, ar was tortured with a lot of metal around him. The reason v wasn't captured was he can use any magic, but the others cannot. Then he wasn't happy with the way of what they did. He came to the battlefield. Took ar as hostage, again. A unleashed his bone magic, but v sliced through it using swords magic, then he changed to bone magic and got A right where he was supposed to hit, everywhere out of nowhere. But n had the hardest magic to face off against. He had mind magic. Whatever he thinks comes to reality and uses that against his opponents. V came hiding found n and used his bone magic, but the effort was wasted because n thought of a wall, metal wall.

revenge

During the war v had broken ni and r out of the
jail they have been sleeping in, but v himself was captured
during the escape route.so r came in killed a and ar, again
(they were healed) ni freed v and r was still fighting n but
ni stabbed n from the back using his well-known space
magic. R's fire magic was out. While all three kings of the
ruynery kingdom were still being healed.

poverty

The best inventory guy r headed out to make a better castle out of stone and wood. He found stone and wood. Then he crafted wood into dumb swords and the stone, he converted into a castle.

But v went and found a lot of wood pickaxes, swords, axes, shovels and a lot more. So, what they did was those homeless in their country, r made at least 25 wood houses for the homeless people and gave each 10,000 crudes their

blood moon

As it was said in the ancient books of when the kingdoms were together, a blood moon would appear once in two months. V ,r and ni were not alarmed of this as n broke into the country, he had said he came in peace to alarm us that there is a blood moon, a portal would appear out of nowhere, but in order to go into that portal they would need an amulet, a gold encrusted amulet. Luckily for v, he had thirteen bars of gold, lapis lazuli and emerald. But the problem was that they needed iron, which r had, the last thing they needed was red stone and diamond which they had and crafted into an amulet which helped into going in the portal, but only one could go through it. V went for Merndend and n went for Ruynery. As v went through the portal first for the merndend people he found a whole different world.

all about the blood moon

2000 years before these people were born, on a specific day, a blood moon appears. Every twelve months a blood moon will appear six times. If the blood moon is called carragjha, it means that the blood moon is deadly and that if a person comes out during a carragjha, it is said that they are cursed. The other blood moon stragajha, means "blessed time". As it was, the day v and n went into the portal the day or blood moon was called a stragajha. On a carragjha, weird things start to appear, that is why when a carragjha appears, you must stay inside.

golems

As v had entered, he first had saw a sign saying BEWARE OF THE HIDDEN GOLEMS. V hadn't listened to the sign, a few minutes later n showed up, but this time the sign said beware of the hidden golems. which no one really saw or cared about it, as v collected iron, he was headed back home until a sword was thrown at him he looked to his left, it wasn't n for it had been a golem. He darted through to the exit. As for n had. Already left for the exit as he killed every single golem except for that one.

invasion

As both countries had braced each other for the war, but the war wasn't about their military defenses it was about two more countries unknown to both ruynery and merndend. As the war was going on both countries decided to help a country by giving, ruynery had the bright idea to help them, but that country took it is in a weak way that they are too weak that they need help, so they also declared war on ruynery, in the end after the war, all the countries divided into a lot of space between the two region. This is how it looks like now.

unhappy

Since the land had been split into many parts most of the countries had been unhappy by splitting as there has been more rebels than they have thought. As the land of one island split into four parts, it was a food chain and as the people of ruynery had sent spies to the countries that have rebelled against ruynery and merndend.

power

With the power that the countries had, they could have the power to destroy the whole world, but the leader of one of the unknown countries had drained himself in power he let ni kill him, and each person had a last straw. If they had drained themselves too much in power they could face death, as the countries reunited into once again, called strey, they reunited to have one land. The belief that everyone had that they could reunite both lands under the power of all six kings. But with this we couldn't guarantee rebels.

n thinks of a scheme

When the countries reunited, n called v and a for an important meeting, which was nothing about poverty and the economics, it was leaving r n and ar behind in the dust but what n didn't say was what he said now 3,2,1. At the moment it didn't make sense but for then they would follow with what happened. N said what happened would not affect the country's wealth, health, economic and GDP. But it would affect the three kings. On the world map strey is located here

team up

As the three teamed up v wasn't sure whether he should do this or not, but in the end, it happened
Even though he didn't like it he wanted it. So, the plan was v had to distract r and ni while n and a would kidnap them while ar is unaware, when he is sleeping v would shoot a tranquilizer dart for extra sleep. But someone was unaware and let their guard down

the scheme

The plan had started. V was talking about economics, ni heard a rustle he spoke up and just when he was about to check cameras, job finished. V shot the tranquilizer dart perfectly on the neck to kidnap ar. As n, a and v were cheering n told not to let their guards down as the hostages were swearing it up at the three who betrayed them.it was them who killed pigs and cows to give them food, but as n told not to leave their guards down something happened at night.

betrayal

In the morning a found himself in a weird place with skulls. He thought it was a dream, but it pained too much to be a dream. Spanking, whipping, flogging slapping, hitting, biting, assaulting and killing. All happening in front of him, a nightmare to happen in front of him. He begged to himself to wake up, but the security guards called him to go into a truck, when he was in the truck, he was shot with a tranquilizer dart. And when he woke up he saw through that the nightmare was real.

locked up

When a woke up he found himself in a cell. He pounded on the cell wall thinking someone would answer, and sure enough, he was right. But it was his best friend who betrayed him, n locked him, ar ni and r in that cell. The people in the cell were mad at v, because they didn't expect this from

Such a wise, kind, and noble man. That wise kind and noble man became a betrayer who didn't appreciate what his friends did for him. So instead of becoming a full-on betrayer, he became a. half betrayer. Every time n went to get pig, v and the others would plan to escape the area, and they found a way, but the first time they tried they failed but the second

Ar joins

As they were formulating a plan for the locked in people to get out, they found a way, but that way got screwed up when a big announcement came out this announcement was ar joining the nv becoming nvar. The plan got destroyed because ar would snitch if v even had talked to him about anything.so instead v had a bright idea or plan or whatever you like to call it. The plan was when n went out to hunt for food, they would free the prisoners.

escape route

As n went to hunt for food, v gave the key into the hands of the devil, ni who unlocked the door and went forward. But at that moment n returned to kill all the remaining jail people, first he drowned most of them before he was stabbed in the back by v, as n was sent to heaven, the god of devils showed n the way of who was who, v was lucefrio, n was sent back with shocking news, v wasn't just lucefiro, he knows the power inside of him but never uses it. It was said in the ancient scroll that if the king of a kingdom has a devil in him, he would be possessed with a tremendous amount of power. But v is a kind man who doesn't use powers like that. People like n are obsessed for the type of power v has, only an idiot wouldn't use such an immense power, said n

mini betrayal

As soon as n came back from the underworld his first aim was to betray all his members, but first he would betray v before betraying everyone in the kingdoms. So, he asked why to v, he said he didn't feel like himself and that the "devil" inside of me. N had realized that from the underworld there was a connection to v, so he quickly killed v because v would not have the devil if n hadn't stabbed him, so v came back without the devil and when he saw n, he took two haladies out of his pocket for safety but n surrendered before v could even pierce his flesh. And so v took him back to the jail where everyone rebelled against n and was happy with v betraying n by stabbing and capturing him

better betrayal

The next day v went to give n his daily food, but he wasn't in the jail, which was astonishing for v because v put in a lot of effort to catch n and all that effort went in vain and was flushed down the toilet in a second. But he wouldn't let his effort go to waste so the second he stepped out he found n, ni came out of nowhere to fight and suddenly it became a war between the good of mankind and the bad ones, v shot a bow onto n's leg and he was going pretty slow, then suddenly we were drowning n had a speedboat and he left a bomb there, but he decided it would be no fun so he took us on his boat, shot tranquilizers at the five , and left them on an island.

stranded on an island

As they were left on an island, they had to hunt for food, they had to build shelter, but v suggested we build a boat. It took more than 27 days to make a boat for 5 people. And when they started the boat, they realized there was no oil, they had built an electric boat that had needed oil they had to dig deep for oil. Ar had found oil, but he dug to deep and on top of that he was like two foot three, so they had to pull ar out if the pit that he himself had dug. When they pulled him out and took the oil to the boat, he put the oil in the boat, and they started their trip back home.

back to home

As they were lost in the middle of nowhere, ar found something there, luckily it was land, but the boat crashed into a rock because they were entering into a reef, r took out a bow attached to a string. Everyone clinged on to him as they made it back home safely, as they were checking for injuries, r with a knee niggle, ni with a hamstring and a with a muscle tear, so for that they had to rest before thinking what to do to the betrayer, n

thinking of what to do to n

After a world full of nonsense, they started to formulate a plan against the devious n. but by then they wouldn't know if n had any treaties with anyone because when v opened the world map he was shocked to see what he just saw. He announced the devastating news of n as only v knows about this.

v, r

ni

a

ar

n

so the plan was the easiest plan, declaring a 5 v 1

knowing

When v found out that n was hiding in the Faroe Islands
they immediately took a flight straight away, knowing that
they had the advantage over n
But the route is different. The route is the weirdest yet
most affective plan
And by luck that was at his house.

serial killer

When they arrived at n's mansion, they saw through the window that he was not alone, he had company, with the name Steve, he would serve n for the rest of his life until he dies, they had realized with that kind of immense power, they needed more support than just 5 people. So, they started making calls to get ready for the attack and sure enough, it started another war that wasn't supposed to start but still started because of the puny man's arrogance

playing a game

They were locked into a room designed into their personal fears, for r, its his parents running away from him r had found a way past it by taking an axe and breaking the doors, v was locked in a coffin until he had to break out of it using his bare feet. A was losing to everyone in everything until he got so mad, he banged his head on something that opened the door for him, for ni it wasn't a room it was a nightmare that was presented, his brother was n, but n left him when he was two, ni couldn't believe his eyes. When he punched his brothers face and that was the key to escaping.

peace love and war

When an outbreak of anger and hatred is there, there will never be peace until the problem is really solved in every way. In this case, it isn't just anger riding on this war, its love, reputation, and many more things, but this war had started with a bow and arrow piercing the Steve's blood, but they weren't happy with that, the serial killer sent a shuriken and a katana at ni, but the shield of r blocked the shuriken. Then v took two haladie's out of his pocket and launched it at n, but any way the haladie would have pierced him if it had hit him, but out of luck it didn't hit him then a used bone magic which could have worked if Steve hadn't done a move to almost kill a. Then it became a one vs one between a and Steve, but the outcome was something no one would respect because this isn't what someone wouldn't hear later on during the war, v found the news of a and by that time, they had retreated.

endbreak

As everyone was trying to kill the two, the backup came, the former merndend army came and fell within a span of five minutes. Then n dispatched a flash of knives at everyone, that's when v did the same with his haladie's, but then, v realized something, he took the bow then he took a haladie, he aimed and fired it at Steve, "revenge for a's death", v spoke up as he was fighting with haladie's, katana's, shuriken's, nun chucks ,grappling hook arrows, swords and bullets. As the last target was n v launched eight haladies at n and he sliced his arms off, ni finished n with a stab to the heart and that was the end to the great war that had been going on for at least more than five years between these two enemies, with 4 casualties and 2 injuries, strey once again was a great country and the war repetitions was more than 40,000,000$.

a new era

After all of what happened they had finally decided to be at peace after such a big war that has just ended, the country's currency crude. 1 crude is equal to 90USD. And now the country's economy, GDP and many more things are at its highest rate after the war, we still respect those who died in the war.